# To

A

Curated by
**Giorgia Di Pancrazio**
**& Katherine E Winnick**

beautifully
rising from the beggar's hut–
a kite

~Kobayashi Issa

To Live Here

Edited & curated by
Giorgia Di Pancrazio & Katherine E Winnick

Cover watercolour, logo and illustrations

Cover design & layout by Stuart Beveridge

ISBN 978-84-09-52816-5

# To Live Here

## A Haiku Anthology

## From The Editors

There is a sense of intimacy and immediacy to haiku that is difficult to capture in any other form of writing. In this anthology, we have sought to create a space where readers can immerse themselves in the sights, sounds, and emotions of the world we inhabit. As co-editor of *To Live Here*, I am thrilled to be able to share the work of so many talented poets who have offered their own unique perspectives on what it means to be alive in this moment.

~Katherine E Winnick

*To Live Here* emerges from a strong need to represent and unite the voices of poets from different parts of the world under a single theme: home. It is my pleasure, as co-editor of this anthology, to take the reader from the familiarity of a spice shop to the foot of the majestic Mount Fuji on one of the most captivating explorations of the five senses.

~Giorgia Di Pancrazio

# Foreword

The Wee Sparrow Poetry Press, founded by Claire Thom, showcases the talents of poets from around the globe, "trying to make wee ripples of kindness in a crazy world." This anthology, curated and edited by Giorgia Di Pancrazio and Katherine E Winnick, explores the theme of 'home'. In the call for submissions, Giorgia and Katherine encouraged writers "to think about earth as our shared home, our connection with nature and the urban environment, and how climate change is affecting us and our habitat."

Over one hundred and fifty poets across the globe took the challenge to heart and delved into ‘home’ as both a physical place and a psychological and emotional dwelling within ourselves. They address how the existential threat of climate change, the loss of natural environments, war, and social injustice, affect our contemporary sense of ‘home’.

From different cultural and personal perspectives, the poets paint a diverse portrait of ´home´ which presents a rich, complex and satisfying collection of haiku. *To Live Here* will warm your heart, stir your frustration and anger, and create inspiration and hope.

I was moved by many of the poets' personal and intimate narratives about their experience of home.

Keiko Izawa of Japan writes about the remembrance of youth:

town river–
a cherry petal raft
drifts into my youth

There are many heartfelt poems about family:

winter hearth
warming my heart
dad's eyes

~Patricia Hawkhead, UK

R. Suresh Babu from India vividly depicts the sensuousness of home:

India spice shop–
the aroma of home
in the glass jars

But, homes may also be filled with pain and loss:

under the eaves
of the foreclosed house–
hornet's nest

~Ruth Holzer, USA

There are the unfortunate among us without homes as described by Jack Granath of the United States

April freeze–
a bedroll in the bushes
by the railroad tracks

In contrast to the personal sense of home, the pithy and funny poem by Birk Andersson of Sweden scolds us for our blindness about the ongoing threats to the planet we share:

beach bottles–
we don't get
the message

Many haiku explore grief and loss:

remembering
the good old days–
a bare tree

~Vandana Parashar, India

In this eerie poem, Brendon Kent, the British haiku poet, confronts us with our place in a degraded world:

am I waiting
for my rebirth too?
skeleton tree

Amidst the coldness of the modern environment, several poets remind us that something as common as a dandelion may reclaim the most lifeless places:

city sunrise–
a dandelion grows
in concrete

–Farah Ali, UK

Daya Bhat of India points us towards the beauty of birds in our urban world:

lake sunset
swans on the edge
of the skyline

Yet with these challenges, the potential for awakening and rejuvenation awaits us:

dry pond
life awaits
the splash of water

~Emma Alexander Arthur of Norway

In a classical nature haiku, poet Randy Brooks of the United States calls our attention to the simplicity and miracle of a turtle waiting to be discovered:

duckweeds
a silver dollar turtle
walks on water

Interspersed throughout the collection, a number of poets explore the effects of political unrest, war and dislocation. Barbara Anna Gaiardoni of Italy evokes the tragic consequences of war in eight words:

rose garden–
a mass grave
in the city

For many a home is not just a physical place but a psychological phenomenon:

new identity
I am called a refugee–
my name anglicised

~Gene Groves, UK

In spite of the throes of conflict, Lakshmi Iyer of India describes the heart wrenching persistence of nature:

homecoming–
Siberian cranes' cry
above the war zone

*To Live Here* accomplishes its mission to illuminate what it means to be 'home' in the 21st century.

I'll leave you with Michele Rule's lovely poem:

coming home–
light shines through
the kitchen window

The proceeds from *To Live Here* will be donated to Salford Loaves and Fishes, a charity in the UK supporting people who are homeless or at risk of homelessness.

May we all see the light!

~Bruce H. Feingold, USA
Chairperson of The Haiku Foundation Touchstone
Awards & author of *everything with an asterisk*

blossoming far way
my roots are growing older
spring calls me again

Eldris Con Aguilar, The Netherlands

city sunrise–
a dandelion grows
in concrete

Farah Ali, UK

winter sun –
paint peels
on the window ledge

Michelle V. Alkerton, Canada

sold house–
the memories
orphaned

Bakhtiyar Amini, Germany

saezuri
a hermit thrush trails
the height of oaks

Rupa Anand, India

beach bottles–
we don’t get
the message

Birk Andersson, Sweden

deer island
by the bay of dreams
deserted

N. T. Anh, Vietnam

dry pond
life awaits
the splash of water

Emma Alexander Arthur, Norway

sandy beach
turtles lay clutches of eggs
off-shore breeze

Francis Attard, Malta

spice shop–
the aroma of home
in the glass jars

R. Suresh Babu, India

across fallow fields
hum of motorway traffic
paled by skylark song

Angela Bailey, UK

spring blossoms
a displaced child
finds his mother

Topaz Bay, UK

moving house–
I carry with me
the song of a skylark

Mona Bedi, India

the caricature opens a lotus flower

Jerome Berglund, USA

lake sunset
swans on the edge
of the skyline

Daya Bhat, India

the old dry river
still fresh the fishing stories
of my grandfather

Mirela Bràilean, Romania

over the middle
of the browning meadow
yellow butterfly

Ed Brickell, USA

after the rain
on the road again–
a snail

Marc Brimble, Spain

spring summoned the robin throat trills

Jade Brooke-Langham, UK

duckweeds
a silver dollar turtle
walks on water

Randy Brooks, USA

searching for
cloud-patterned
smoke-filled sky

B. L. Bruce, USA

animals unknown
vanishing before our eyes
extinction unseen

Sarah Cain, UK

clouds dance
upon the ceiling
moon roof

Jillian Calahan, USA

stalking heron
a shutter flashes
hazy dawn

Erin Castaldi, USA

climate change
the place you recognize
the place you don't

Andrea Cecon, Italy

glaciers' melting–
the polar bear is born
at the zoo

Marta Chocilowska, Poland

acanthus
swollen roots
fill the pot

Ken Cockburn, Scotland

the aged cherry tree–
now and then a ground dove
rests in her branches

Gillena Cox, Trinidad

cypress trees
the scent
of my ancestors

Alvin B Cruz, Philippines

pruning roses–
talks of rebuilding
the city

Maire Morrissey Cummins, Ireland

empty buildings
lining city streets
the homeless

Tracy Davidson, UK

swallows depart
sunlight fades in the west–
darkness fills the house

Sarah Das Gupta, UK

glass tank
turtles basking in sunshine–
two eyes look out

Anna Dean, Australia

a night's sleep
the desire to drink coffee
in his mother's house

Refika Dedic, Bosnia and Herzegovina

yellow sun, blue sky
your pink lips smothering mine–
all life is colour

Ryan Diaz, USA

I bring home
the smell of lake clouds
deep water

Fiona Dignan, UK

my hometown
is the same–
I am not

Jovana Dragojlovic, Serbia

climate change–
building a snowman
at Easter

Ana Drobot, Romania

a wingbeat
the wren is deep in blackthorn
- hammering heart

Susannah East, UK

be still like a tree–
the world will move around you
close your eyes and breathe

Rob Edwards, UK

fog on the lake
water becomes sky–
last days of winter

Eavonka Ettinger, USA

golden rice shoots
under Fuji's eye—
farmer stops for tea

Louis Faber, USA

rose and lavender
line the walkways in our yard
the clouds overhead

Cristina Fariñas, USA

Kamo River banks–
paper lanterns flood the sky,
stars returning home

Thomas Farr, UK

desert cliffs
the shadow of a raven
carries dad home

Bruce H Feingold, USA

mushroom foraging
dad racing ahead
knife in hand

Agnieszka Filipek, Ireland

in and out of
a stump hollow
wood wasps

Helen Gaen, UK

rose garden–
a mass grave
in the city

Barbara Anna Gaiardoni, Italy

garden guests glide down
confetti crusts bless the lawn
no-one goes hungry

Bridget Gallagher, UK

an old man rocking
in spring's warm sunlight–
jasmine's fresh scent

Al W Gallia, USA

April freeze–
a bedroll in the bushes
by the railroad tracks

Jack Granath, USA

heat wave
adding salt
to the curry sky

John S Green, USA

new identity
I am called a refugee–
my name anglicised

Gene Groves, UK

slow tick of the clock
the old house fills with stories
- father's war

John Hawkhead, UK

winter hearth
warming my heart
dad's eyes

Patricia Hawkhead, UK

fresh leaves unfurl–
woodpeckers knock
holes in trees

Jane Hanson, Italy

ripples in hot wind
dust before the flames–
home held too tightly

Terence Hayes, Wales

geese on the beach
the shade of the pine trees
already taken

Joy Heath, UK

open window–
a plastic bag up a tree
shivers in spring winds

Melanie Hering, UK

under the eaves
of the foreclosed house—
hornet's nest

Ruth Holzer, USA

air dried sheets
scent of summer
in my bed

Vanessa Hope, UK

morning meditation
the last cloud drifts over
the horizon

Edward Cody Huddleston, USA

last haven
the knot of tadpoles
in a puddle

Marilyn Humbert, Australia

a gust of wind
the street cleaner
takes a break

Mona Iordan, Romania

homecoming–
Siberian cranes' cry
above the war zone

Lakshmi Iyer, India

town river–
a cherry petal raft
drifts into my youth

Keiko Izawa, Japan

holding up
the world's gardens
root people

Roberta Beach Jacobson, USA

meeting the dusk
by a mustard field
homeward journey

Govind Joshi, India

empty streets
cherry trees in full bloom—
Fukushima

Deborah Karl-Brandt, Germany

mango season
the pull of granny's home
grows stronger

Vipanjeet Kaur, India

am I waiting
for my rebirth too?
skeleton tree

Brendon Kent, UK

after centuries
eagles taking residence
in Ireland

Noel King, Ireland

pink clematis...
still tracing the face
of our childhood home

Robert Kingston, UK

from a forest
to the soup bowl
tiger in free fall

Ravi Kiran, India

mockingbird sings me
into the garden
this time

Craig Kittner, USA

on the skylight
rain waves smearing
shadows of bare trees

Tricia Knoll, USA

the path home - each tree hums its own story

Krzysztof Kokot, Poland

starry night–
the mountain village becomes
crickets' song

Nadejda Kostadinova, Bulgaria

morning light above the dew dragonflies

Seth Kronick, USA

pond ripples
from the minnows
the heron missed

Chris Langer, USA

coming home
my slippers
where I left them

John Lanyon, UK

hummel moths migrate
south for the winter–
silk cocoon emptied.

Ken Le'Marchand, USA

a ladybug
mistakes me
for a flower

Luke Levi, USA

the shape of home
a bluish restless shadow
keeping vigil

Sylvia Loh, Germany

winter's veil lifts
hummingbird and spider negotiate
threads for shelter

Margaret Lonsdale, Canada

baby's head
nestled under chin—
home

Mirjam Mahler, Germany

dustbins
full of paper cuttings–
earth day celebration

Devoshruti Mandal, India

fewer bees this year a chill of petals

Clare Martin, UK

friendship garden...
shortening the path
of a caterpillar

Richard L. Matta, USA

on the verge a stork stepping out

Fokkina McDonnell, The Netherlands

three cornered field
the generations
who farmed here

Julie Mellor, UK

my ancient soul friend
snow
I feel you slipping away

Maryam Mermey, USA

grandma's tales...
picking out zucchini seeds
around the table

Daniela Misso, Italy

flowers without petals–
a bee searches
for another universe

Mircea Moldovan, Romania

fresh bed sheets
flapping in the wind–
lilac scent

Emma Mooney, Scotland

in the canal
under the moonlight
a frog is in song

Peter Morriss, Scotland

rationing water
every swimming pool
a reservoir

Tina Mowrey, USA

sailing across
the windswept loch–
swan's feather

Kenneth Mullen, UK

grass that's seen millions
the earth remembers each face
of her residents

K. G. Munro, Scotland

morning rush hour–
dandelions shaking
around the bus stop

Krzysztof Mxchx, Poland

solitary tree
in a talkative forest
looking at its feet

Nora Nadjarian, Cyprus

over a turlough
a cloud of migrating birds
their murmurations

Sean O'Connor, Ireland

craving black seeds–
childhood teddy bear
eyes miss home

Toreh O'Garro UK

a butterfly moves
to the open-winged heron–
harvest moon

Maeve O'Sullivan, Ireland

forgetting street names
in the old neighbourhood
autumn fog

John Pappas, USA

remembering
the good old days–
a bare tree

Vandana Parashar, India

sun-dappled path
a golden swallowtail
lights up

Sarah Paris, USA

outdoor drinkers–
white plastic bag
spreads its wings

Ciarán Parkes, Ireland

the smell of orchids
the only thing remembered
at her funeral

Kenneth Pearson, USA

bronchiole branches
guiding me through the forest
lost in nature's arms

Adele Louise Pennington, UK

angler and fish
unaware of each other—
muddy green pond

Ian Petrie, UK

a song of the wind
a dance of the prairie dust–
nomad's home

Ksenia Alessandra Petrova, Mexico

springtime–
trail of petals leading back
to the beginning

Becky Potter, USA

in the gutter
a thousand stars
shattered

Dan Price, UK

sun-kissed mountains
rise from morning mist–
postcard from home

Sally Quon, Canada

old village banyan
history
on hanging roots

Kala Ramesh, India

lark sparrow lands
on the trembling branch—
endangered species

Valentina Ranaldi-Adams, USA

deep winter
the widow's porch light
always on

Bryan Rickert, USA

peach blossom–
blooming with the same joy
as last year

David Rodrigues, Portugal

no watch and no map
along the path of pines
a finding

Ellen Rowland, Greece

tattered fishing nets
abandoned little boats
the river weeps

Avinash Roy, India

coming home–
light shines through
the kitchen window

Michele Rule, Canada

cherry blossom drifts
on a puff of exhaust fumes
a raven cries out

H J Russell, Scotland

blowing wind
teases the lantern–
frogs croak

B. S. Saroja, India

new day
he wraps the samosas
in old newspaper

Minal Sarosh, India

a beach of sea stars...
this crisis
that didn't make the news

Julie Schwerin, USA

drought
at the bottom of the well
the moon is waning

Slawa Sibiga, Poland

spring forest
treating my darkness
with birdsong

Tomislav Sjekloca, Montenegro

deserted farm
echoes
of sheep

Neil Somerville, UK

asbestos shingles
a cowbird chick
covered with ants

Joshua St Claire, USA

seventeen years' sleep
cicadas risc from the earth
into barrenness

Margaret D Stetz, USA

new neighbours
the sparrows seem to
get along with the bulbuls

Sankara Jayanth Sudanagunta, India

another town
perhaps some day
- dandelions

Kaushal Suvarna, India

disused car park–
herring gulls
sunbathe in lines

Sarah Tait, UK

the spider's web
mid-morning coffee
with my new neighbour

Marie-Therese Taylor, Scotland

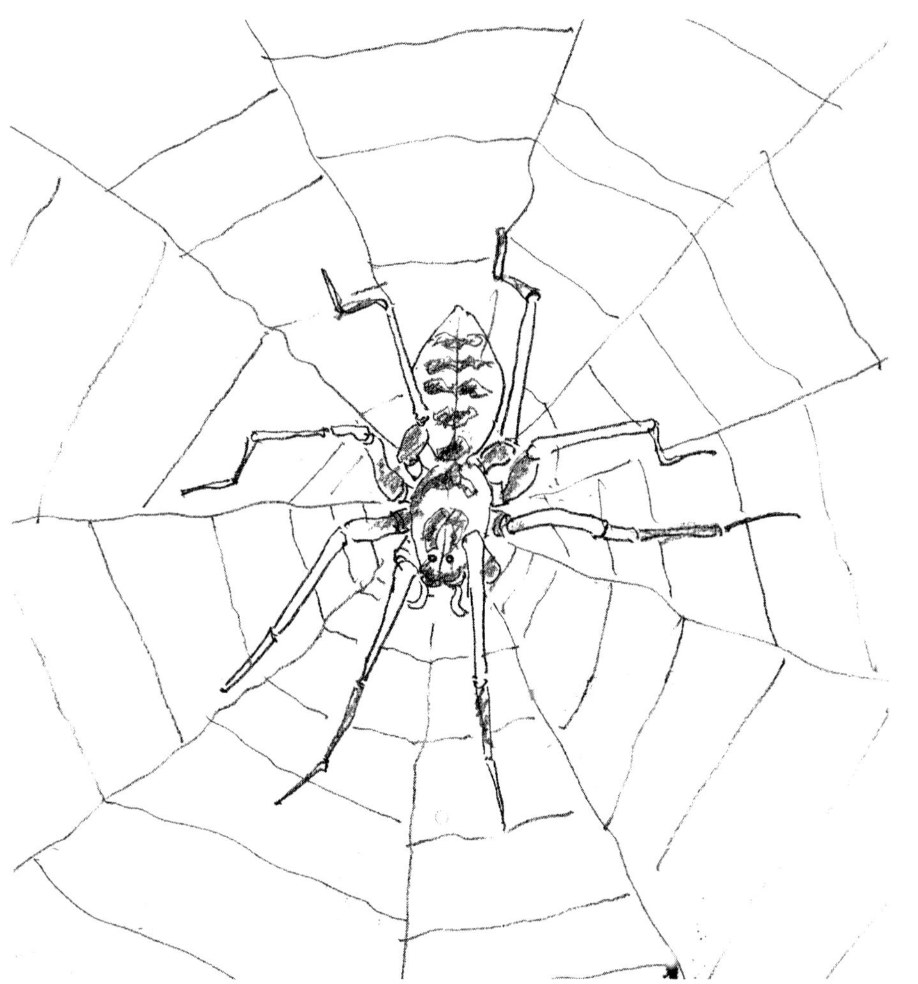

cicada's song
as morning sweats with fury—
the rising sun burns

Charlie Thomas, Malaysia

little souvenir
carried home from Mt. Fuji–
rock inside my boot

David Thorndale, Japan

spring storm
more bees
than flowers

Kristina Todorova, Bulgaria

rhubarb harvest
a taste of snow and rain
in my hands

Xenia Tran, Scotland

return after years
through the keyhole
the same light

Zuzanna Truchlewska, Poland

derelict house
comprising memories
- still standing

Ilias Tsagas, Greece

not only me
moving north
bee orchid

C.X. Turner, UK

wildfires burning
everything turns to dust–
home is gone

Christian Ward, UK

the beggar's cup
empty– these days
it's all contactless

T.W. Warrpos, Spain

the waterfall's spray
blurs both of our sunglasses–
I drop to one knee

Michael Dylan Welch, USA

rhubarb leaves
unwrinkle to catch
spring sunbeams

Tyson West, USA

golden summered shards
blues amongst chalk hills
drifting to anywhere

Jake Williams, UK

zen heron
sitting by a river
full of fish

Tony Williams, Scotland

in the privet hedge
outside our living room—
house sparrows chatter

Juliet Wilson, UK

lake bed
from his blue guitar
songs of rain

Jamie Wimberly, USA

last child
leaves home
call of the nighthawk

Valorie Broadhurst Woerdehoff, USA

late night party–
waiting at the house door
father's worries

Nitu Yumnam, India

dawn in an airport
step in and out of
life's suitcase

Azida Zainal, Malaysia

Thank you to all the poets included in this anthology for trusting us with your words. The Wee Sparrow Poetry Press is honoured to give your haiku a home.

Thank you also to Giorgia Di Pancrazio and Katherine E Winnick for all their hard work receiving submissions and selecting the haiku for this collection, to Bruce H. Feingold for writing such a wonderful foreword, to Stuart Beveridge for designing the gorgeous front cover and for formatting the final manuscript; and to Colin Thom for his beautiful illustrations.

www.theweesparrowpoetrypress.com

*We are far more united*
*and have far more in common*
*than that which divides us.*

*~Jo Cox MP, 1974 - 2016*

Made in United States
North Haven, CT
02 August 2023